THE EiFFEL PYRA

BY

AZiZA NiZARALi

ILLUSTRATED BY LANA USSMANE

AND SUBHAAN NiZARALi

DEDICATED TO:

MY FRENCH COUSINS NOAH, LAYNA AND JAYDEN WHO I
MISS AND LOVE VERY MUCH.

Contents

Chapter One – Messy Mary

Mr mummy woke up. He looked around the room nervously. He could feel his heart racing. "Where am I?" he cried out. Suddenly he remembered everything.

A sausage dog called Doogie had appeared in Egypt in a time-travelling grandfather clock and Mr Mummy had helped him get home to the year 2020 in England! And now Mr Mummy was stuck at Doogie's house where you couldn't make sandcastles or draw views of pyramids on walls and many other fun things.

Mr Mummy went and woke up Doogie, who was snoring louder than ever. "Wake up Doogie! Open those eyes, come on! Wake up!" Doogie opened his eyes and did a loud, worried bark!

"This will help you," said Mr Mummy. He undid some toilet roll from around his body and shouted: "TELTER! STRONG SPELL! OUFE!" and waved the toilet paper over Doogie's head. He then explained to Doogie that it was magic and that he would be able to talk now.

"Thank you," said Doogie. "Wait, what?! It's a zombie! A zom…."

"Shshshsh!" whispered Mr Mummy. "Remember who I am?"

Suddenly Doogie remembered. "Oh! Oh no! No! No! No! We have to get you back home!" he said.

"No, that shall take way too long and I'm clock-sick! Wait, maybe I can dress up as a little boy so I can blend in?" asked Mr Mummy.

"Perfect idea! Let's go to Penny's (Doogie's owner) little brother Peter's room," cried Doogie.

"LET'S GO!!!" yelled Mr Mummy.

Peter was fast asleep. Doogie and Mr Mummy tiptoed into his room and Doogie emptied the cupboard. Doogie threw some clothes at Mr Mummy who put them on in five seconds.

Mr Mummy walked into the living room where Penny was making breakfast. "Um… hello! Who are you?" asked Penny. She picked up a glass of milk.

"I am Mr Mu… um, no! I mean Mr… Mr, m, m, Mary! Mr Mary!"

Penny was so confused that she dropped the glass of milk. "Ahhhhh! Um, Mr Mary, why are you covered in t-toilet paper?"

"Um… uhh… hello-ween?" said Mr Mummy.

"You mean Halloween? It's in seven months!!!" said Penny. She bent down to pick up the glass she had dropped, but her head hit a Coco-Pops box which fell over and Coco-Pops spilt everywhere. Penny picked up a bottle of orange juice which had a missing lid and went over to the other side of the kitchen to get a cloth and find the missing lid, but she slipped on the milk that she had spilt and the orange juice that she was holding also spilt everywhere.

Penny was so frustrated that she screamed louder than ever.

Peter came running into the room and slipped on the orange juice.

"Peter! Are you okay?" asked Penny.

"I can't find my favourite football top," said Peter.

"Wait a second!" shouted Penny angrily. "Mr Mary! Is that Peter's favourite football top you are wearing?!" She sat up, frowning.

"Y-y-ye-n-n… I mean y-y," began Mr Mummy. Doogie ran into the room barking louder than ever. He ran out again with Mr Mummy not too far behind.

"MY FOOTBALL TOP!!!" yelled Peter.

"I'll buy you a better one, but first let's clean up this mess!" said Penny. "I'll have a chat with Mr Mary's parents."

Chapter Two – The Still Statue

When Mr Mummy and Doogie got back to Doogie's room they started discussing what to do next.

"I know, maybe you could pretend to be a statue!" said Doogie.

"PERFECT! PERFECT IDEA!" yelled Mr Mummy.

Suddenly they could hear footsteps coming towards them.

"Quick! Pretend to be a statue!" whispered Doogie. Mr Mummy took off Peter's clothes and did a funny pose.

The door opened and Penny came in.

"I see you've got a statue of a zombie, Doogie?" she said as she looked at Mr Mummy with a confused look on her face. Doogie nodded and barked. "But you're scared of zombies. Let's put this in the shed and take it out again on Halloween," said Penny as she picked up Mr Mummy and took him down the marble staircase, through the side door, round the corner, through the gate and finally into the shed.

As soon as Penny left the room Doogie started to panic. "Halloween is in seven months," he shouted. "I must save Mr Mummy!"

Doogie ran towards the big brown shed, but it was locked, so he jumped through the window and walked towards a big box that said:

Halloween

Decorations

It took Doogie seventeen whole minutes to open the box. When he had finally opened it he saw Mr Mummy lying in the middle still doing his silly pose.

"Come on," said Doogie. "We're going back in time. Let's get you home."

"I'd love to," said Mr Mummy.

Chapter Three – The Royal Queen Mummy

Soon they were both inside the time-travelling grandfather clock.

"Which year do you wish to visit?" it asked. Ten numbers from 0 to 9 appeared in front of Doogie. He put in the number 1 and then wagged his tail.

Mr Mummy was behind Doogie and Doogie didn't know that he had accidentally tickled Mr Mummy with his tail. Mr Mummy began to laugh and he knocked into a loose windowsill. The windowsill began to shake and a bouncy ball that was on it rolled off and towards the clock, hitting the number 8 that was in front of Doogie three times.

"You are going to the year 1888," said the grandfather clock. Neither Mr Mummy or Doogie heard this. Mr Mummy had heard some thunder, which he was scared of, so he had blocked his ears, and Doogie didn't listen properly. He thought the grandfather clock had said that they were going to the year 1300 so he was not worried.

The grandfather clock spun into a tornado... and they were gone.

Once they landed Mr Mummy ran out of the clock and did an excited scream. He opened his eyes and looked around, but what he saw was not what he expected...

People were walking around and shaking hands. There was no sand on the floor!

"THESE, THESE P-P-PEOPLE! THEY HAVE TAKEN OVER EGYPT," yelled Doogie "We have to find you some clothes Mr Mummy! Then you can dress up as a boy and find a pyramid to hide in for the rest of your life!"

"The rest of m-my life?" asked Mr Mummy.

"YES!" said Doogie. "Let's go get you some clothes!"

Soon they were hiding round the corner of a restaurant called La Maison Royale.

"Ok," said Doogie. "Do you see those jackets hung up on those hooks? Take one and put it on, then meet me by that big tree over there."

Mr Mummy nodded and went into the posh-looking restaurant. He walked past a beautiful lady who looked like the Queen. This was strange because on the news it said that the Queen was visiting Paris for five weeks, but they were in Egypt?

Mr Mummy walked towards where the jackets were hanging, trying not to be seen as he knew if someone saw him they would run and scream.

He looked at the jackets. There was a green one with buttons and a hood, a red one with no hood and a zip, a beautiful pink, glittery cardigan, and a green one that had buttons and no zip. Mr Mummy liked zips. The red one didn't have a hood, and it might rain. The pink sparkly one was too girly! Then he saw the perfect one, it was warm, beautiful, cosy and cool. It was labelled:

Queen

The Royal Family

Please do not touch!

Mr Mummy didn't see the writing. He grabbed the jacket and ran to Doogie at the big tree. Doogie stared at him.

"ARE YOU CRAZY?" he yelled. "That's the Queen's jacket! Everyone will think you're the…" Before he could finish his sentence about a hundred people came towards them holding cameras and microphones.

"C'est La Reine," said a lady wearing a blue scarf.

"Where is your crown?" asked a news reporter.

"I can't believe it's the Queen!" shouted a man with a camera.

"Cela est si excitant," called a girl.

"S'il vous plait puis-ie avoir un autographe?" asked a boy.

"RUUUUUUUN!!" yelled Doogie. "They all think that you are the Queen!!!"

Doogie and Mr Mummy ran, leaving all the news reporters, children and adults behind.

After running for almost six minutes they found themselves standing in front of a giant pyramid-type structure.

"Wow!! I think it's a giant pyramid! I'll climb it and live in it forever!" said Mr Mummy.

"HURRY UP!" yelled Doogie. "The grandfather clock is going to get bored and then grow legs and run away in four minutes!"

"I'll miss you! You're my best friend! Goodbye," said Mr Mummy.

"Goodbye," said Doogie. He hugged Mr Mummy. "I'll miss you too and I promise I'll visit you," he ran off to the grandfather clock which was around the corner, while Mr Mummy began to climb the steps of the giant pyramid.

Doogie ran into the grandfather clock and typed in the numbers 2020 and then off he went.

Chapter Four – Pyramide de Paris

Soon Doogie was home. He was sad because he couldn't talk any more, but happy because he was home. He walked towards Penny.

"Doogie! Doogie! Doogie! Guess what?!" said Penny.

Doogie did an excited bark.

"Next Thursday we are going to Paris, and we will see the Queen and this really cool building called the Eiffel Tower. We are going for two weeks! Let me show you a picture of the Eiffel Tower, I know you've never heard of it before."

Penny sat down next to her computer. Doogie jumped onto her lap.

"Aha," said Penny. "Look, Doogie, I've found a picture of the Eiffel Tower, look on my computer screen."

Doogie looked up at the screen. He did a worried bark. On the computer was a picture of the same tower Mr Mummy had thought was a giant pyramid and decided to live in forever.

"This is in Paris!" said Penny.

Doogie felt more worried than ever. He had left Mr Mummy alone in Paris, in a year he didn't know, in an unsafe tower!

Doogie was going to save Mr Mummy before his amazing holiday…

But that's a whole other story!!!

THE END

PRODUCED BY

JACK's JOURNEYS PRESS

ON BEHALF OF

AZIZA NIZARALI

JACK'S

JOURNEYS

BRINGING YOUR CHILD'S STORY TO LIFE...

WWW.JACKS-JOURNEYS.COM

Printed in Great Britain
by Amazon

79772605R00018